Tower Block Blowdown

J. Burchett and S. Vogler
Illustrated by Caroline Sharpe

Cambridge Reading

General Editors
Richard Brown and Kate Ruttle

Consultant Editor
Jean Glasberg

PUBLISHED BY THE PRESS SYNDICATE OF THE UNIVERSITY OF CAMBRIDGE
The Pitt Building, Trumpington Street, Cambridge CB2 1RP, United Kingdom

CAMBRIDGE UNIVERSITY PRESS
The Edinburgh Building, Cambridge CB2 2RU, United Kingdom
40 West 20th Street, New York, NY 10011-4211, USA
10 Stamford Road, Oakleigh, Melbourne 3166, Australia

First published 1998
Reprinted 1998

Printed in the United Kingdom at the University Press, Cambridge

Typeset in Concorde

A catalogue record for this book is available from the British Library

ISBN 0 521 63746 5 paperback

Cover design by Heather Richards

For the children of Gainsborough and Mountnessing primary schools

Other Cambridge Reading books you may enjoy

Leaving the Island
Judith O'Neill

Captain Cool and the Robogang
Gerald Rose

Half of Nowhere
Richard Burns

A True Spell and a Dangerous
Susan Price

Other books by J. Burchett and S. Vogler you may enjoy

The Proper Princess Test

Ghost Goalie

Save the Pitch

‘BOOM!’ read the poster in the bus shelter. ‘TOWER BLOCK BLOWDOWN! One O’clock Today. Viewing Point – Alexandra Park.’

Peter made his way to the corner of the park. It wasn’t every day you saw a building being blown up. There was a big crowd behind the safety fence. A group near him had champagne bottles – all ready to pop with the explosion. He couldn’t see any of his friends. They’d said they were going to be there. Perhaps they were on the other side.

Everyone else seemed to have someone to chat to. He caught snatches of a conversation between two old men.

"Do you remember the first block they tried to blow up here? Only half of it went down."

"Yeah, the papers called it the Leaning Tower of Wickney."

"Typical Council – always making a mess of it. Remember the houses that used to be here? Even in 1940, Hitler only needed one bomb to flatten them."

Peter couldn't wait until one o'clock. He wished his friends would turn up. As he looked round for them, he noticed a girl. She was about his age. She was on her own, too. She was thin and pale and she was wearing a nightie. She was pulling faces at people in the crowd. Peter laughed, but no-one else seemed to notice. He stuck his tongue out at her. She rushed over and stared him in the face.

"Can you see me?" She waved her hand in front of his eyes.

"Of course I can," he said. "I . . ."

"You *can* see me," she gasped. "You're the first one!"

Peter wondered if she was a bit potty – and he wasn't going to stay to find out.

"Look," she said importantly, "I don't want to scare you. I'm very friendly. I'm not evil or

anything . . ." – she paused dramatically –
" . . . but I'm a *ghost.*"

Peter tried to speak, but she carried on.

"You don't believe me – I'll show you."

Nearby was a man sitting on the grass, drinking a beer. The girl went up and pulled his hair. He took no notice. When he put his

can down on the ground, Peter saw that his arm passed right through her.

She came skipping back.

"There you are," she said. "Awesome, isn't it? I died up there, you know." She pointed dramatically at the empty tower block.

"Eleventh floor, where the hole is. I expect you remember the gas explosion. I'm the girl who died. It was in all the papers. There was a picture. It was taken last year, when I got my football medal. I was top scorer for the Wickney Under Eleven side. Chelsea Roberts – aged nine."

"Chelsea? That's a funny name . . ."

The ghost wasn't listening.

"It was over so quickly, I didn't feel a thing. Then afterwards, when I realised I was staying up there, I thought it might be a laugh. Haunting people and all that. Rattling chains, howling now and again. You know – like in the old films. But I found I hadn't got any chains, and they moved everyone out of the block. I've been so lonely on my own."

"Why did you stay up there, then?" asked Peter. "I'd have . . ." But the girl wasn't used to having anyone to talk to and she was going to make the most of it.

"One day, the builders came in and I thought – great! Here's someone to spook.

But they walked right through me. Then I heard them saying they were going to demolish the tower. I knew I had to get out. So I'd be free. I mean – otherwise I might have been stuck haunting a pile of rubble. BOR-ING! So I managed it. I got out." She looked extremely smug. "I used all my super-duper, extra-special spectral powers and I floated through that door – and it was locked then!"

She pointed to the open door at the bottom of the tower.

"I feel a bit odd now I've done it. Anyway, stop nattering. I want to see what's going on."

Peter was angry. So what if she was a ghost? What was so clever about going through a door? Surely all ghosts could do that. She might think she was special, but it didn't give her the right to tell lies either. Fancy pretending she was called the name of his favourite football team.

"I don't believe you," he said.

She turned round.

"What you said. About scoring all those goals."

"Well, I'll show you then, smartypants. Here's the medal to prove it."

She put her hand to her neck.

"Oh no! I've left it up there. Quick, let's have a look at your watch. Twenty-five to one. Nearly half an hour. Plenty of time."

She ran through the safety barrier as if it wasn't there.

"Hang on a minute!" shouted Peter.

"I've got to get it," she yelled back. "I always wear my medal. You stay put."

"You haven't got time," called Peter.
"This watch . . ."

But the girl was too far away to hear. She ran down the path towards the tower block. The crowd was getting into a party mood. Some people were singing along to the Wickney Steel Drum Band. One or two were even dancing. Peter watched the girl go.

Good riddance, he thought.

But as he saw her disappear into the building, he began to worry. He didn't actually know what happened if you got blown up twice. Perhaps she *would* be stuck . . .

No-one saw Peter slip through the safety barrier and run across the deserted area. He stopped at the open door and looked up. It felt as if the tower was slowly leaning over him. He hated heights. He couldn't go in – but he had to. It must be nearly one o'clock. He had to tell her – his watch was no use. It always said twenty-five to one. It had been broken for ages.

He ran inside and started up the stairs.

"Oi!" he yelled. "You haven't got time. Come back!"

Up and up he ran. Some of the floor numbers were broken, others were missing. He lost count. He didn't dare look out of the windows. He was higher than he'd ever been in his whole life.

He stopped. Perhaps this was the eleventh floor. There was silence. He wandered through the empty rooms. It was spooky. Cracked floor tiles, peeling wallpaper and old posters. There was no sign of the girl.

He found a door. 'Fire Exit – Tenth Floor'. Tenth floor! He was wasting time. Even if she made up stories about playing football he had to find her.

He raced up one more flight of stairs. Now he could hear something. A door stood open. The sound of crying echoed eerily around him. It must be the girl. He hoped it was the girl. He stepped into the room and stopped just in time. Beyond the broken floor there was a gaping hole. He felt the cold air on his face. Before he had time to think, he looked down. He could see the green park and the tiny people below. The bulldozers looked like miniature dinosaurs, lying in wait.

Chelsea's

Peter had forgotten the horrible dizzy feeling he'd always had when he climbed too high. He turned away quickly. His head was spinning. He'd been stupid to come up here. Then he saw the sign on the door. 'Chelsea's Room. KEEP OUT!'

He could see the girl now. She was huddled in the corner, sobbing.

"I've lost my medal. It fell out of my hand. It went over the side."

From far below came the loudspeaker. "Ladies and gentlemen. Trowbridge House will be demolished in three minutes."

"Three minutes?" gasped Chelsea. "I must have more time than that. What does your watch say?"

"I tried to tell you," said Peter crossly, "but you didn't stop to listen. My watch is broken. It always says twenty-five to one." He showed it to her.

"Let's get out of here," said Chelsea quickly. There was no sign of any tears now.

"But what about your medal?" asked Peter.

"I don't want to be stuck here for ever." She glared at him. "I'll do without it."

"Very clever," he said. "The medal that never was. That was a trick, wasn't it. You wanted me to be trapped in the explosion."

"That's a lie," shouted Chelsea. "I didn't know you were following, did I? I told you to wait down there. Why would I want you to be blown up like I was?"

"You wanted someone to share your haunting. You said you were lonely. You *are* evil."

A loud klaxon sounded. They could hear the distant shout of the crowd.

"Two minutes."

"COME ON!" Chelsea yelled. She disappeared down the stairs.

Peter went to follow her, but somehow he felt drawn to the edge, towards the eleven-storey drop. The scene below lurched in front of his eyes. Then he saw a flash of red and gold. Something was caught on a jagged piece

of the concrete floor. It was the medal. Chelsea had been telling the truth all along.

Peter knew he had to get it back for her. But was it possible? He knelt down and tried to grab it. His fingers touched the ribbon. The medal slipped a few centimetres, but caught on a rusty nail. Lying flat on his stomach, his eyes tightly closed, he reached over the edge. He felt around. At last it was in his grasp.

Triumphantly he ran to the door. As he flew down the stairs, he heard the crowd already counting down to the blast.

"Ten . . . nine . . . eight . . . seven . . ."

He dashed past a broken window.

He could hear Chelsea's voice.

"Hurry," she was screaming. "HURRY!"

"Six . . . five . . . four . . ."

Peter took a tremendous leap down the last few steps.

"Three . . . two . . . one . . ."

As he raced to the door, he could see Chelsea outside. He held up the medal.

BOOM! The crowd gasped as clouds of dust burst out of every window. The building collapsed upon itself. It was almost graceful. The dust rose slowly in the air. When it cleared, all that was left of the tower block was a huge pile of rubble.

The crowd stood around for a while. They drank their champagne. Then they went home. The show was over. No-one saw the little ghost standing by the rubble, crying.

Chelsea cried as if her heart would break. The boy was probably dead, and all because she hadn't listened to him. He'd be a ghost now, and he'd be very angry.

Then she heard someone whistle. She looked up. Peter was climbing down towards her. A piece of concrete rolled down and passed right through him. He was laughing.

"Crikey!" he called. "That was exciting. Just wait until I tell my friends." He waved the medal at her. "Look what I've got for you."

"What are you so pleased about?" she shouted at him. "You and your stupid watch. Don't you know you're dead?"

Peter smiled.

"Of course I know I'm dead," he said. "I know more about being dead than you do. I've been dead for years. My watch stopped when Hitler's bomb hit us. Twenty-five to one, Tuesday, 8th October, 1940. I tried to tell you but you were such a big mouth."

For once Chelsea had nothing to say.

"Me and my friends have had ever such a good time – playing Spitfires and Messerschmitts. And football. 'Specially football. Wait till I tell them what happened to me. Here, take your medal." He pushed it into her hand and ran off towards some boys who had appeared on top of the rubble.

"Hey, Tommy! . . . Douglas! . . . Bill! . . . I've been blown up again!"

Chelsea watched him go. She was free of the tower block but now she felt lonelier than ever. She wandered off towards the empty

park. She didn't know what else to do.

"Oi!"

Chelsea heard the shout. But it couldn't be for her. No-one could see her. It was probably one of the workmen.

"Oi, Chelsea!"

She turned round. It was Peter. He ran up to her.

"D' you want to play football?" He grinned. "We need a centre forward."